Dear Parent:
Your child's love of reading starts here!

Every child learns to read in a different way and at his or her own speed. Some go back and forth between reading levels and read favorite books again and again. Others read through each level in order. You can help your young reader improve and become more confident by encouraging his or her own interests and abilities. From books your child reads with you to the first books he or she reads alone, there are I Can Read Books for every stage of reading:

SHARED READING
Basic language, word repetition, and whimsical illustrations, ideal for sharing with your emergent reader

BEGINNING READING
Short sentences, familiar words, and simple concepts for children eager to read on their own

READING WITH HELP
Engaging stories, longer sentences, and language play for developing readers

READING ALONE
Complex plots, challenging vocabulary, and high-interest topics for the independent reader

ADVANCED READING
Short paragraphs, chapters, and exciting themes for the perfect bridge to chapter books

I Can Read Books have introduced children to the joy of reading since 1957. Featuring award-winning authors and illustrators and a fabulous cast of beloved characters, I Can Read Books set the standard for beginning readers.

A lifetime of discovery begins with the magical words **"I Can Read!"**

Visit www.icanread.com for information
on enriching your child's reading experience.

To parents who will be reading
this book to your children—
RAP IT!

*I'm Rappy the Raptor
and I'd like to say,
I may not talk
in the usual way.*

RAPPY

and His
Favorite Things

To Tamar —D.G.

To three of my favorites:

Caleb, Grady, and Brylie. —T.B.

I Can Read Book® is a trademark of HarperCollins Publishers.

ISBN 978-0-06-225271-5 (pbk.)
ISBN 978-0-06-225272-2 (hardcover)

19 20 21 22 23   SCP   10 9 8 7 6 5 4 3 2 1   ❖   First Edition

RAPPY
and His
Favorite Things

by Dan Gutman

illustrated by Tim Bowers

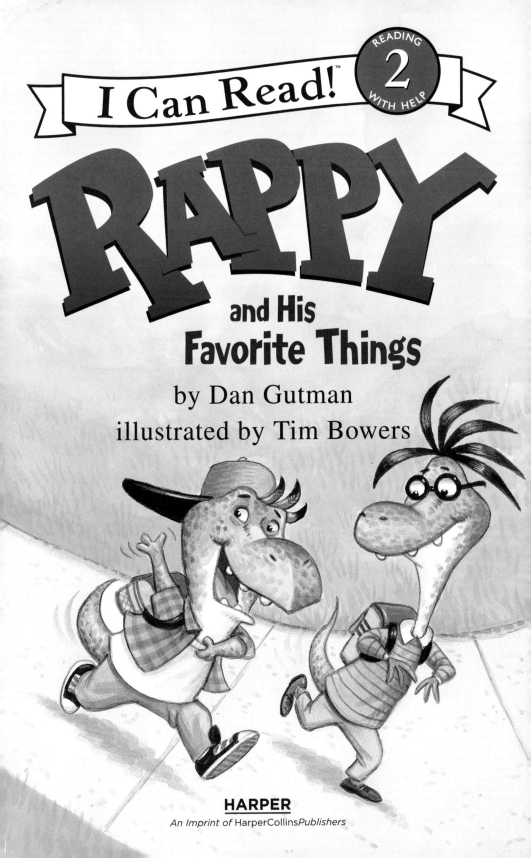

HARPER

An Imprint of HarperCollinsPublishers

Got a little time?

Try talking in rhyme.

All you have to do

is go line by line.

I'm rapping on the street.

I'm rapping on a plane.

I'm rapping on a mountain.

I'm rapping in my brain!

We got to school

and put our backpacks in our cubbies.

Then I asked my teacher,

"Are we doing social studies?"

"Are we gonna do math?"

"Are we gonna do spelling?"

"Are we gonna take a bath?"

Everybody was yelling.

"Quiet!" Mrs. Hooperlooper said.

"Let's do something else instead."

She said "Quiet down" again.

"Get out a notebook and a pen."

What are we gonna do?

I really wanna know.

Can we go outside?

Can I play in the snow?

Can we sing a song?

Can I throw a ball?

Can we play Ping-Pong?

Can I climb the wall?

Then Mrs. H. began to speak.

She said, "Kids, it's Poetry Week!"

Put a Poem
in Your Pocket
Day

But poetry is *really* hard!

Can't we play in the schoolyard?

I'd rather climb up a skyscraper

than stare at a piece of paper.

I don't have a clue
how to write a poem.
I don't know what to do.
I want to go home!

13

I was feeling kind of queasy.

Mrs. H. said, "This is easy!

Think of something that you like.

Playing ball. Riding a bike.

Reading books or watching TV.

Drawing pictures. Climbing a tree.

Maybe dancing is your thing,

or maybe you just like to sing.

It's okay to make a mistake.

We all do that, for goodness' sake.

I'll accept whatever you make,

but the best poet wins a cupcake!"

"Let's get to work," our teacher said,
"Just use the words stored in your head.
Soon the bell is going to ring.
Write about your favorite thing."

This was sure to be my doom.

Silence fell upon the room.

We were just a bunch of fakes.

None of us would get cupcakes.

I thought that I might take a nap.

But instead I started to rap. . . .

I like pizza and chicken wings.

These are a few of my favorite things.

Standing on my head.

Jumping on a bed.

Wishing on a star.

Playing a guitar.

Hanging with my pets.

Flying in a jet.

Wearing funny hats.

Feeding my two cats.

Playing lacrosse.

Eating applesauce.

Flying kites
and pillow fights!

All my friends were keeping the beat.

They started rapping in their seats.

"I like going sledding

or sometimes to a wedding!"

"Buying clothes! Squirting a hose!"

"Smelling a rose! Going to shows!"

"Playing with dogs! Catching frogs!"

"Buying a dress! Making a mess!"

"Seeing plays! Catching rays!"

"Snowy days! Mayonnaise!"

"Climbing up an apple tree!"

"Spelling bees! Water skis!"

"Virtual realities!"

Alex rapped about his vacation.

Aidan rapped about his dalmatian.

Mia rapped about trampolines.

Joey rapped about Halloween.

Judy rapped about the Bahamas.

Chris rapped about warm pajamas.

Hannah rapped about jumping rope.

Connor rapped about cantaloupe!

We were rapping on the floor.

We were rapping on the ceiling.

We were rapping on the door.

We were rapping with feeling.

We rapped about school.

We rapped about flowers.

We rapped about teachers.

We could have rapped for hours!

Hannah was humming.

Niko was drumming.

None of us had seen it coming.

It kind of took me by surprise.

I couldn't believe my ears or eyes.

We were in a state of shock.

Suddenly it was three o'clock!

It was the most amazing thing. . . .

The dismissal bell began to . . .

RRRRRRING!

Now it was time for us to go home,

but we hadn't written a single poem!

I thought our teacher would be mad,

but she looked like she was glad.

We all began to clap and snap

when Mrs. H. began to rap. . . .

"You may like to jump.

You may like to sew.

But I want to tell you

something that I know.

Maybe you're a queen.

Maybe you're a king.

But rapping and poetry

are the same thing!"

"So if you have a lawn,

you'd better mow it.

When you get a toy,

you want to show it.

If you have a ball,

you need to throw it. . . ."

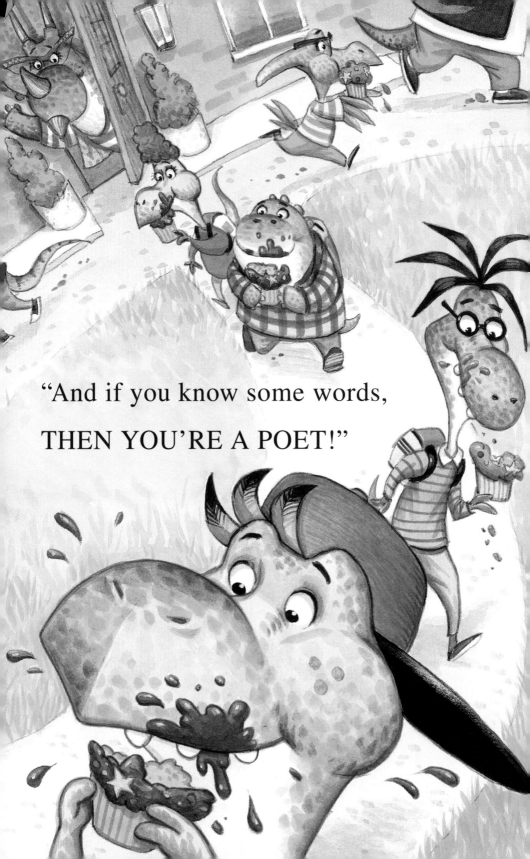

"And if you know some words,

THEN YOU'RE A POET!"